Nature

STICKER STORIES

DOGS and PUPPIES

Illustrated by Karen Lee Schmidt

GROSSET & DUNLAP • NEW YORK

Copyright © 1998 by Grosset & Dunlap, Inc. Illustrations copyright © 1998 by Karen Lee Schmidt.
All rights reserved. Published by Grosset & Dunlap, Inc., a member of The Putnam & Grosset
Group, New York. GROSSET & DUNLAP is a trademark of Grosset & Dunlap, Inc.
Published simultaneously in Canada. Printed in Singapore.
ISBN 0-448-41747-2 A B D E F G H I J

Dogs come in all shapes and sizes. Some are pets. Others work as police dogs, fire dogs, or watch dogs.

LABRADOR RETRIEVER

Wolves are related to dogs.
They live together in groups
called wolf packs.

Sometimes hunters take dogs along on the hunt. Hounds, terriers, and retrievers are good hunting dogs.

Herding dogs help out on the farm.
They keep sheep and cows together
and move them from place to place.

pages 2-3

DALMATIAN

DACHSHUND

JACK RUSSELL TERRIER

LABRADOR RETRIEVER PUPPY

DOBERMAN PINSCHER

GERMAN SHEPHERD

COCKER SPANIEL

LABRADOR RETRIEVER

PUG

WOLF PUP

pages 4-5

WOLF

WOLF

WOLF PUP

WOLF

WOLF

WOLF PUP

WOLF PUP

WOLF

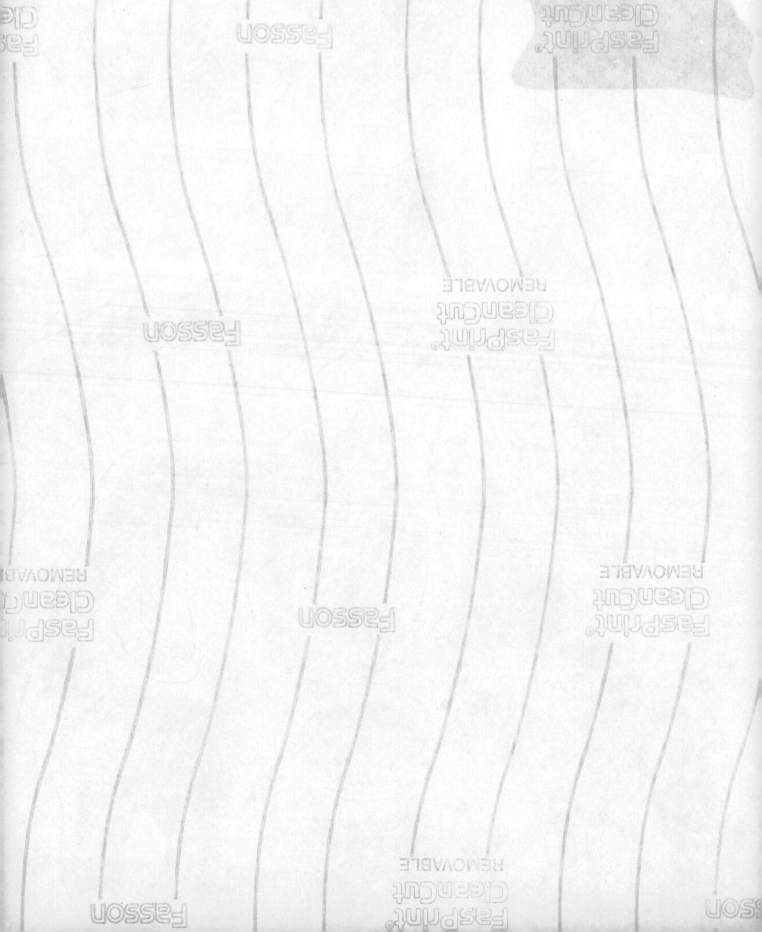

HUNGARIAN VIZSLA

WEIMARANER

BEAGLE

GERMAN SHORTHAIRED POINTER

BLOODHOUND

BEAGLE

ITALIAN SPINONE

IRISH SETTER

IRISH SETTER

MANCHESTER TERRIER

pages 8-9

GERMAN SHEPHERD

COLLIE PUPPY

COLLIE PUPPY

COLLIE PUPPY

COLLIE

BORDER COLLIE

SHETLAND SHEEPDOG

BORDER COLLIE

WELSH CORGI

OLD ENGLISH SHEEPDOG

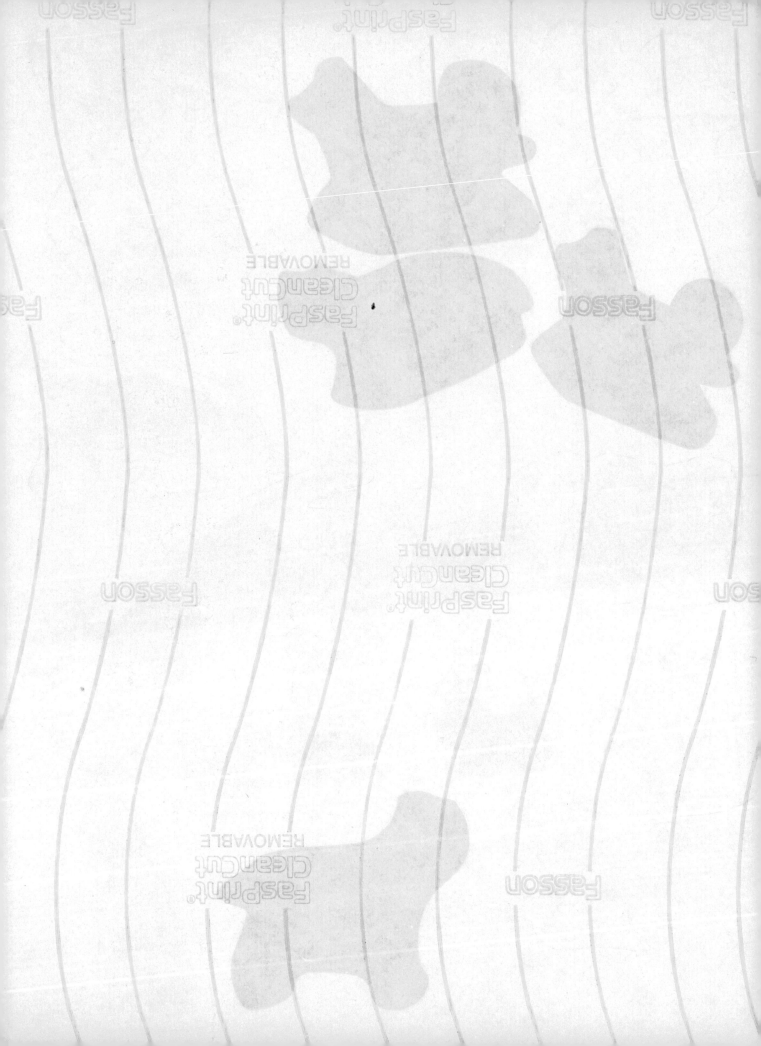

pages 10-11

SIBERIAN HUSKY

SAMOYED

SAMOYED

SIBERIAN HUSKY

pages 12-13

CHOW CHOW

SPRINGER SPANIEL

GREYHOUND

LABRADOR RETRIEVER

SCOTTISH TERRIER

CHIHUAHUA

AIREDALE
TERRIER PUPPY

LABRADOR
RETRIEVER PUPPY

POODLE

BOXER

NORWICH TERRIER

SCOTTISH TERRIER

BICHON FRISE

POODLE

BASSET HOUND

CHESAPEAKE BAY RETRIEVER

ST. BERNARD

COLLIE

NORWEGIAN ELKHOUND

GREAT DANE

GREAT DANE PUPPIES

SPRINGER SPANIEL PUPPY

GOLDEN RETRIEVER

SAMOYED

LABRADOR RETRIEVER

MALTESE

COCKER SPANIEL PUPPIES

SKYE TERRIER

COCKER SPANIEL

DALMATIAN

Sled dogs have thick fur to keep them warm. Put together your own dog team and join in the race!

ALASKAN MALAMUTE

ALASKAN MALAMUTE

SIBERIAN HUSKY

City dogs love the park, where they can run and play and meet other dogs.

Every dog is a winner at this dog show!

AIREDALE TERRIER

Dogs are part of the family.